MY
LITTLE ALIEN
FRIENDS

SUE EXTON

PUBLISHED INTERNATIONAL ARTIST AND AUTHOR.

All the illustrations in this book are taken from original paintings by the author.

Grosvenor House
Publishing Limited

All rights reserved
Copyright © Sue Exton, 2023

The right of Sue Exton to be identified as the author of this
work has been asserted in accordance with Section 78
of the Copyright, Designs and Patents Act 1988

The book cover is copyright to Sue Exton
Illustrations copyright © Susan Exton 2023
All planet images copyright © NASA 2023

This book is published by
Grosvenor House Publishing Ltd
Link House
140 The Broadway, Tolworth, Surrey, KT6 7HT.
www.grosvenorhousepublishing.co.uk

This book is sold subject to the conditions that it shall not, by way of
trade or otherwise, be lent, resold, hired out or otherwise circulated
without the author's or publisher's prior consent in any form of binding or
cover other than that in which it is published and
without a similar condition including this condition being imposed
on the subsequent purchaser.

This book is a work of fiction. Any resemblance to
people or events, past or present, is purely coincidental.

A CIP record for this book
is available from the British Library

Paperback ISBN 978-1-80381-374-5
Hardback ISBN 978-1-80381-375-2
eBook ISBN 978-1-80381-376-9

TABLE OF CONTENTS

A TEACHING BOOK FOR CHILDREN: PLANETS OF OUR SOLAR SYSTEM

1. INTRODUCTION 1
2. HOME PLANET 3
3. IN THE LIBRARY 5
4. DIGGY TAKES CONTROL 8
5. MY FRIEND MOG 10
6. PLUTO 13
7. IN MY IMAGE 14
8. NEPTUNE 16
9. IT'S IN THE CLOUDS 17
10. URANUS 19
11. CARPET GRASS 21
12. SATURN 23
13. LIQUID PEOPLE 25
14. JUPITER 27
15. THE STACKERS 29
16. MARS 31
17. KING SPRING 32
18. EARTH 35
19. HUMANS 37
20. VENUS 53
21. JELLY WALLS 54
22. MERCURY 59
23. TEAPOT 60
24. THE SUN 63
25. TEACUP 64
26. GIFTS 68

1. INTRODUCTION

Now, I have found that in a child's mind, fact and fiction can be one and the same thing.

It's only when we grow up that the fiction fades and the facts become all too real.

We must learn not to blinker children with science, but to open their eyes so they can see for themselves all the wonders it holds.

With fiction, we must allow a child's mind to explore for itself all the wonders of freedom of thought.

Hopefully, I have combined just enough of both to keep a child interested, while also teaching them a little about our solar system, so that they will want to go on and read more.

I believe the best thing to hear in life is children laughing, and the next best thing is a good bedtime story.

2. HOME PLANET

Far away, beyond the stars, is a small planet called Swoke.

On the planet Swoke lives a very special alien called Diggie. He's rather short, with big brown eyes, the strangest big, floppy ears, his body is covered in fur, and his feet are so big he seems to wobble when he walks.

Diggie is very interested in the stars and planets. He often listens to radio signals and picks up all the information he can from them so that he can plan his next big adventure into space. Now, Diggie's radio is a very special radio that can pick up signals from far across the universe and way out into space.

He would often tour the stars and planets, looking for rocks to add to his vast collection, in his little spaceship which he calls I-I. I know that sounds a little strange, I-I, but that's because the first time he switched on his new satellite system and requested information, all the answers he received ended every time with, "I-I, Captain." So I-I seemed like the best name he could think of at that time for his little spaceship.

Diggie is called a geologist – someone who studies rocks. Diggie is not his real name, but as he is always digging for rocks, his family gave him that nickname. Diggie's real name was Fred, but he didn't like it. He much prefers to be called Diggie, so that is what everybody calls him.

One morning, just after breakfast, he tuned into a radio signal from a planet called Earth.

How strange! he thought. *It's coming all the way from another solar system.* It talked about the coming of the millennium, and how all the planets in that solar system would line up and stand to attention on the fifth day of May in the Earth year 2000.

Now, Diggie had no concept of days, weeks, or millennia, so he wasn't even sure if the alignment had already taken place or not, but it did all seem so exciting.

Diggie lived with his best friend Mr Whisky-bee, who was so strange to look at as he looked just like a round ball sitting on a cushion that was floating about four feet off the ground. But Mr Whisky-bee was a very special friend, with magical powers only he had. But I will tell you all about those later.

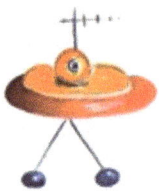

3. IN THE LIBRARY

Diggie was intrigued about this alignment of planets, so he rushed to his bookshelf and took out a little red book that contained all the information he had about the planets of Earth's solar system.

"Mmm," he muttered to himself. "Not much to go on here, but never mind." It was there and then that he decided he would go and find out more for himself. He didn't want to leave Mr Whisky-bee alone, though.

In the past, they had visited other planets in their own solar system, but this would be a very special long trip, with so many unanswered questions, so Diggie took the little red book to show Mr Whisky-bee. After a short conversation, it was settled that they would go together as soon as possible. Packing started in earnest.

They would need Diggie's little space trailer for all the rocks they intended to collect on their way, so they packed the tools into the trailer, then they packed the spaceship I-I. It wasn't very big, but just had enough space for some food and the two of them.

They had no idea what they would find, but this would be their biggest adventure ever. Mr Whisky-bee thought it would be a nice idea to take with them a gift to give to all the aliens who lived on the new planets they were about to visit. Yet what kind of gift do you give an alien? After some thought, it was decided in the end that Diggie and Mr Whisky-bee would make some gold and silver bells.

Diggie asked for two extra bells, so he could hang one up in his own spaceship and give one to his friend Mr Mog, who lived on a nearby planet.

It took Mr Whisky-bee no time at all to make them, with his magic spinning. This was one of those special things Mr Whisky-bee used his magic for. As he spun around and around, the cloud that he sat on would produce the items he was thinking of. It was so clever! Diggie had always known about Mr Whisky-bee's magic powers, but it still surprised him that Mr Whisky-bee could produce such perfect items.

A few days later, their excitement was building. Diggie was a very good organiser, so all the checks needed to be carried out carefully. He checked the fuel, and then the engine for oil, and only when all the checks were made to his satisfaction and Mr Whisky-bee was ready, was it time to leave.

Diggie and his little spaceship I-I were all good to go, and his trailer was packed with his digging tools so that he could collect a little piece of rock from each new planet in Earth's solar system to add to his collection. Of course, he had also packed his little red book about Earth's solar system, with a very small map at the back of it.

Diggie climbed into the driving seat. Mr Whisky-bee didn't need a seat, so he would just float behind the driving seat and hopefully make a good map reader. But Diggie knew Mr Whisky-bee would often get the maps upside down, so he would need lots of patience if the trip was to go smoothly.

The last thing Diggie did before leaving was to hang his new little gold bell up in his spaceship I-I. Then at last they were ready to go.

4. DIGGIE TAKES CONTROL

Before leaving their solar system, Diggie wanted to go and visit his friend Mr Mog, who lived on the next planet, Hout. There were lots of other planets in Diggie's solar system, but he had explored them many times before, so this time it was just to be the one stop to see Mr Mog, to tell him all about this new and exciting adventure.

It was still a long journey to see Mr Mogg, so Mr Whisky-bee came up with a new game for them to play. Over the years, this was something Mr Whisky-bee was very good at. They had come up with new names for unnamed planets, and they had also renamed some comets.

Comets always left a long tail of gas behind them, so Mr Whisky-bee called them 'fart tails', which always made Diggie laugh every time they spotted one. They would be travelling along quietly, when all of a sudden, if one was spotted, they would shout out, "Fart tail, fart tail!" And whoever called out first would collect a point.

But this time, Mr Whisky-bee's new game was quite different. It involved a cube with little emojis on each face, so they would ask the spaceship's computer to pose a random question, and whoever got the correct answer first was the winner. The other player then had to throw the dice, and whichever emoji image landed on top was the face they had to impersonate.

Mr Whisky-bee did have an advantage, as he could make so many different faces, but poor Diggie had lots of problems making emoji faces. However, as time passed by so quickly, it was always fun when they played games.

5. MY FRIEND MOG

It took almost two days to reach the planet Hout, and Mr Mog was waiting patiently for them. His eyes lit up as the little spaceship touched down in front of him. Mr Mog had to be very careful when he greeted his friends, because he was almost double Diggie's size, with hands as big as tennis rackets.

Diggie climbed down, and stumbled just a little on the last step, but instantly Mr Mog's hands reached out and caught him.

"Whoopsie daisy!" said Mr Mog. "Stopping long?" he asked.

"Not this time," said Diggie, and he then told Mr Mog all about their new adventure.

"Any room for me?" asked Mr Mog, and they all laughed out loud together, because they knew Mr Mog couldn't fit into the tiny spaceship I-I. The three friends talked for hours, had a little supper, and fell fast asleep.

The following day, Diggie and Mr Whisky-bee gave Mr Mogg his silver bell for luck then said their goodbyes and waved frantically as their little ship sprang into the air and high into the stars. It would be almost a year before he would see Mr Mog again, but Diggie had promised to pop in on his return journey to tell him all about his adventure.

Diggie watched in amazement as his ship sailed by the last two planets in his own solar system, and on towards the Earth solar system.

The new stars he saw sparkled in his eyes, and it was with joy in his heart that he looked forward to reaching the very first planet in Earth's solar system.

He pulled out his little red book from under his seat. "The star at the centre of Earth's solar system is called the Sun," he read aloud so Mr Whisky-bee could hear all the details. "The Earth is orbited by eight planets and one dwarf planet."

He turned to the page about the first planet he would reach on his journey through the stars.

Now, I say planet, but Pluto is now better known as a dwarf planet. However, if we count Pluto as a planet, that would make nine stops for Diggie and Mr Whisky-bee, so they had packed nine bells, including one for Pluto.

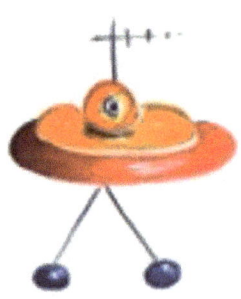

6. PLUTO, THE FACTS

It simply read:

Pluto

Diameter: 2,274 km.

Pluto is the farthest planet from the Sun and by far the smallest.

Pluto's orbit is highly eccentric. Sometimes it is closer to the Sun than Neptune (the next planet in the solar system) and sometimes it is further away. Pluto rotates in the opposite direction from most of the other planets.

Charon

Charon is Pluto's only satellite and has a diameter of 1,172 km.

Pluto and Charon are unique. Not only does Charon rotate strangely, but they both keep the same face towards one another. This makes the phases of Charon, as seen from far away, very interesting.

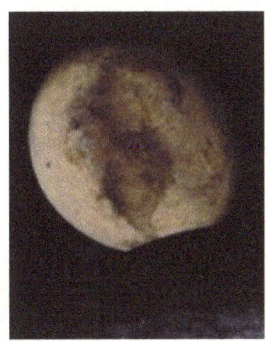

That's not much information, Diggie thought to himself, *and how strange – Pluto spins the wrong way. It doesn't say anything about the beings that live there – I wonder if there are any!*

Diggie was about to find out for himself, as his little spaceship I-I headed to Pluto. Before he knew it, he had landed with a bump!

7. IN MY IMAGE

Before Diggie stepped off the last rung of his ladder, he realised he was not alone, but surrounded by beings so much like himself – small, round, and very inquisitive. It made him feel right at home.

Everyone was fascinated with him and Mr Whisky-bee, and they all started speaking together. "Where did you come from?" they asked. No-one had ever landed on Pluto before, and they were all so interested. They asked question after question, but Diggie was happy to answer them all.

They all seemed like one big family and Diggie felt right at home. As he looked around, he saw that even the homes were just like his own one back on Swoke. They even had the same aerials reaching high into the sky. It didn't take Mr Whisky-bee long to work out that a signal picked up by their aerials must have bounced the signal from Earth onwards to their own planet.

Everyone was so friendly, and they were only too happy to show off their homes.

Diggie explained that he was on a rock collection trip, and when it was time to leave, he asked if he could take a piece of Pluto rock for his collection. They were only too keen to offer him the biggest rock he had ever seen, but he explained that if he loaded it into his trailer, he would never be able to take off! With their permission, he chipped off a small chunk and placed it carefully into the trailer.

He thanked his new friends, and before they left, Mr Whisky-bee reminded Diggie about the silver bell. He unpacked one and handed it over to the lady in the group. She was so happy, throwing her arms around Diggie so tightly that he almost stopped breathing.

Then off they went, high into the skies again, with their new friends calling after them, "Come again some day!"

8. NEPTUNE, THE FACTS

Diggie had been travelling for almost a full day when he caught his first sight of the next planet, Neptune. He quickly pulled out his little book, and turned to the right page and read aloud:

Neptune

Diameter: 49,532 km.

Neptune is the 8th planet from the Sun and the 4th largest by diameter.

Neptune's blue colour is the result of the absorption of red light by methane in the atmosphere.

Neptune's winds are the fastest in the solar system, reaching over 2,000 km per hour.

Diggie paused, after reading his book, because he had never steered his ship through such strong winds before. He was a little afraid, but he was determined to get a rock to add to his collection, so he pressed on. It wasn't easy. Every time Diggie got close to landing, a gust of wind would blow the spaceship right back out into space again. It took many attempts, but finally he made it.

9. IT'S IN THE CLOUDS

What kind of beings could ever live here? Diggie thought to himself, but he didn't have to wait long to find out. As he lifted the cockpit over his head, he and Mr Whisky-bee could hear a whispering noise. He thought at first it was the wind, but looking around, he saw the strangest of beings.

Light and fluffy, each one looked like a little cloud with a face, and they were looking straight at him.

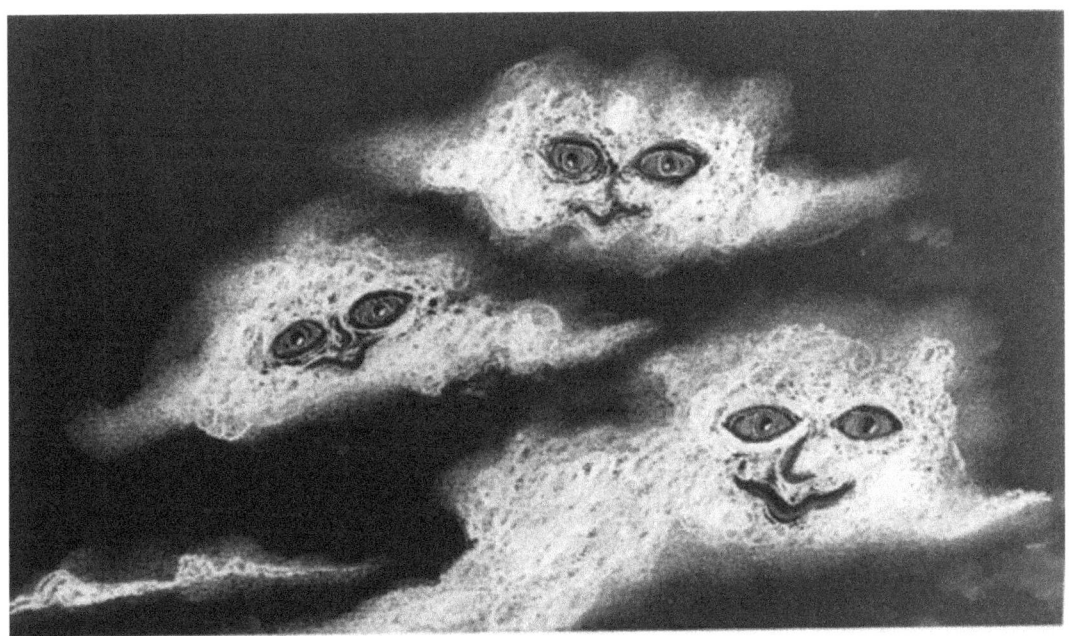

Now, Diggie had seen some strange things in his time, but nothing quite as strange as this. The fluffy things understood every word and were very helpful, showing Diggie where he could collect some rock.

Diggie and Mr Whisky-bee wasted no time in collecting the rock, as they were keen to be on their way before the wind grew any stronger. It was clear on this occasion that a little gold and silver bell wouldn't be the right gift, so Diggie asked Mr Whisky-bee if he had any other ideas.

Mr Whisky-bee suggested a star that he could shoot out above the clouds after take-off, so that it could be seen by all of the fluffy beings and remind them of the visit.

"Oh, how perfect," said Diggie. So a star it was.

They were in a hurry to see the planet Earth, where the original radio signal had come from, so they thanked these strange beings and climbed quickly back up the ladder. Just after take-off, Mr Whisky-bee launched the star, which looked so perfect shining in the dark sky.

Diggie looked over his shoulder back towards the planet Neptune. Those strange clouds' eyes were looking straight up at them, and he could feel the hairs standing up all along his fluffy, furry body.

Once he was back on board and his little spaceship was safely on its way again, Diggie checked to see which planet he would be visiting next.

10. URANUS, THE FACTS

"Uranus," he read out loud from his book. "How exciting! This planet has rings around it."

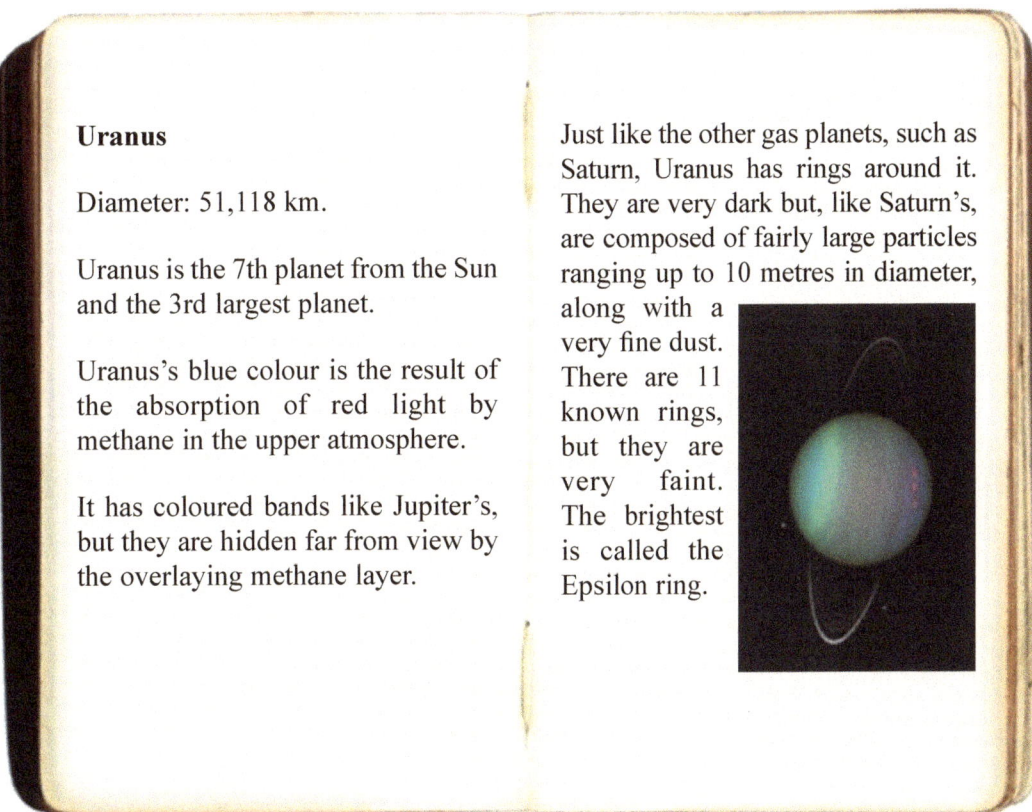

Uranus

Diameter: 51,118 km.

Uranus is the 7th planet from the Sun and the 3rd largest planet.

Uranus's blue colour is the result of the absorption of red light by methane in the upper atmosphere.

It has coloured bands like Jupiter's, but they are hidden far from view by the overlaying methane layer.

Just like the other gas planets, such as Saturn, Uranus has rings around it. They are very dark but, like Saturn's, are composed of fairly large particles ranging up to 10 metres in diameter, along with a very fine dust. There are 11 known rings, but they are very faint. The brightest is called the Epsilon ring.

Diggie and Mr Whisky-bee took their time and slowly slipped through one ring, and then another, and another, just having fun. Finally, they slowly floated down to land – or so they thought.

Diggie turned off the spaceship's engine, but found that the ship was still jiggling up and down.

It was going to be difficult to get out of his spaceship if it kept moving, so he launched his little TV camera eye to find out what was causing all the jiggling.

11. CARPET GRASS

When he saw the pictures from the TV eye, Diggie was amazed. He'd landed on the back of a huge animal! It was pink, and covered in giant oblong shapes of many colours.

Looking out of the spaceship window, he could see lots more creatures, huddled back-to-back, as far as the eye could see. When the markings matched, they looked just like a large, patterned carpet.

Diggie thought it might be unsafe to leave his ship, and although he was a little disappointed, he decided to leave without a piece of rock from Uranus. He opened a little chute on the front of his spaceship I-I, and the TV eye floated back in safe and sound.

Diggie made his way slowly back through the rings. *Oh well, never mind,* he thought. *If I have time, I'll try again on my way home.*

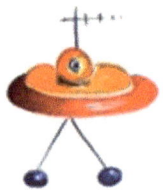

12. SATURN, THE FACTS

Saturn was next. As Diggie and Mr Whisky-bee looked ahead, they could see it approaching in the distance. They were amazed by its spectacular ring system, but couldn't help smiling as they chuckled together and said out aloud at exactly the same time, how much it looked like a head with a hat on.

Diggie's book told him very little about this planet. It read:

Saturn

Diameter: 120,536 km.

It is the 6th planet from the Sun and the 2nd largest.

It is the least dense of the planets. Its density (0.7) is less than that of water.

The rings seem to be composed of water and ice, but they may also include rocky particles with icy coatings.

13. LIQUID PEOPLE

Diggie was very hot when he arrived on Saturn, so he decided to go for a long, cool swim. He knew Mr Whisky-bee couldn't join him, so Mr Whisky-bee looked after the space ship and Diggie went alone.

The water on Saturn was cool, gold in colour, and very inviting. As Diggie splashed about, he noticed how strangely the water behaved. When he lifted his hand out of the water, he saw another hand take shape just in front of him, which appeared to mimic everything he did.

Then, as he slowly stood up, so did an identical Diggie, made of a strange gold-coloured water. The real Diggie began to leave the water, and as he did so, the liquid Diggie stretched out his hand and gave Diggie a gift. Then he disappeared back from where he had come.

It all happened so quickly that Diggie was just a little frightened, but he stayed calm. After a moment or two, he opened his hand, and saw the most beautiful rock he had ever seen. It glittered and shone with reflected light from deep within.

Diggie looked back so he could say thank you, but the mirror image of Diggie had gone. All he could see were the most beautiful sea curls swimming across the surface of the liquid. Diggie had seen sea curls before, because he had seen them on another planet in his own solar system. They were strange little animals, gold and silver in colour, who loved to move in lines across the surface of the gold liquid.

Time was passing, so it was time for Diggie to get dried and return to his spaceship I-I. Before long, he and Mr Whisky-bee were steering through the stars towards Jupiter.

14. JUPITER, THE FACTS

Jupiter was the next planet, and as he approached it, Diggie could see bands and swirls of colour, and a giant red spot on its surface. He reached into his pocket and pulled out his little book again. Diggie knew one fact for sure, and it was that Jupiter was so big you could fit all the other planets in this solar system inside it and still have room left.

Jupiter

Diameter: 142,984 km.

It is the 5th planet from the Sun and the largest planet in the solar system.

It is 318 times bigger than the Earth and twice as massive as all the other planets put together.

Jupiter has a core of rocky material amounting to 10-15 times the mass of the Earth.

The outermost layer is composed primarily of ordinary molecular hydrogen and helium, which is liquid in the interior and gas farther out.

The atmosphere we see is just the very top of this deep layer of water, carbon dioxide, methane, and ammonia. Simple molecules are also present in tiny amounts.

Jupiter's colours correlate with the cloud altitudes: blue for the lowest, followed by browns and whites, with reds for the highest. Sometimes we can see holes in the upper layers and look through to the lower layers.

Jupiter is just about as large as a gas planet can grow. If more material were added, it would be compressed by gravity.

Jupiter has rings, but, unlike Saturn, its rings are dark. They are probably composed of very small grains of rocky material and don't have any ice.

On Jupiter's surface is a Great Red Spot. It is caused by a violent whirling storm that has been raging for at least 300 years.

15. THE STACKERS

On Jupiter, lived the Stackers, who stacked everything they could get their hands on. Their stacks were so tall that they seemed to almost reach the stars. There was building on top of building; it was just so incredible to see. They always seemed to be smiling, and were very pleased to see Diggie and Mr Whisky-bee. No sooner had the spaceship landed than they had arranged a party for their visitors.

The Stackers wore no clothes, and their bodies looked like stacks of different coloured bricks. Even their eyes were square! In fact, the only curved thing about them was the huge smiles that greeted Diggie and Mr Whisky-bee.

The Stackers loved to dance in the streets, and decided to make up a new dance just for their new visitors. They called it the Diggie Jiggle. Diggie was delighted as he watched the Stackers jiggling under the streetlights, and he joined in until the music stopped.

Then one of the Stackers took Diggie's hand and led him to a huge table groaning with food. It was time to eat. As Diggie sat down, he noticed that all the food was also arranged in stacks. There were many shapes and colours, each with a different taste, and all of them were delicious. Diggie had never eaten anything like it before.

After the party, he was so full and so tired that he and Mr Whisky-bee decided to stay the night, and have a good rest.

The following morning, he was ready to set off again bright and early, but not before he gave the Stackers their little silver and gold bell.

As Diggie turned to say goodbye to the Stackers, they gave him a square box. They told him it was the perfect rock for his collection, as it was easy to stack into his spaceship. Diggie was delighted, but the rock was so tightly wrapped in a pretty coloured bow that he decided to open it later, so he popped it under his seat. What Diggie didn't know was there was more than just a rock inside!

Once everything was packed and stored safely inside, it was time for take-off.

16. MARS, THE FACTS

The next planet was Mars, and Diggie's book read:

Mars

Diameter: 6,794 km.

It is the 4th planet from the Sun and the 7th largest.

Although Mars is much smaller than Earth, its surface area is about the same as the land surface area of Earth.

Mars has a very thin atmosphere composed mostly of tiny amounts of carbon dioxide, nitrogen, and argon, with traces of oxygen and water.

On parts of Mars, a weak magnetic field exists.

17. THE KING SPRING

As Diggie landed on Mars, he could hear some very strange noises, so he slid out of his seat and began to climb out of his spaceship. He heard something like a whisper and a very squeaky noise, but when he looked around again, he saw nothing on the ground. He looked again, and there they were. They each looked just like a spring with a round ball bouncing up and down on it.

"Hello, my name is King Spring," said the strange creature at the front. "What's yours?"

"Diggie."

"Well then, Diggie, what can we do for you?"

"I'm on my way to Earth," Diggie explained, "and as I go, I'm gathering rocks for my collection."

"That's a strange thing to collect, if you ask me," said King Spring, "but I'm only too pleased to help passing visitors."

It was at that moment Mr Whisky-bee floated out of the spaceship, the springs all took a bounce backwards, then King Spring jumped forward.

"I think I know you. You're Mr Whisky-bee."

"Well," said Mr Whisky-bee. "We meet again." His words took Diggie by complete surprise.

"It's been a long time. Do you remember when we first met, Mr Whisky-bee, you told me how to oil my spring with oil from the planet Kewe. That planet is still in your solar system, isn't it?"

"Of course," said Mr Whisky-bee.

"Well, you were right when you said it would make bouncing much more fun, and you were right when you said it would make the bounce so much higher!"

At that point, King Spring looked upwards towards the hills behind them. Diggie could see lots of young springs bouncing over hilltops, having so much fun in the bright, breezy, sunny day.

Everyone had a good laugh at the young springs; they were bouncing everywhere, and it was such a funny site to see.

"Well now, Diggie, I think you were telling me all about the rocks you wanted to collect. We have so many different ones here on Mars. Have you got any one rock in mind?"

"Not really, just a rock. Any rock will do," replied Diggie.

"Oh, I think we can do better than just one rock," said King Spring, and he turned to ask one of the other springs to fetch something for him. When the spring returned, he was holding something like a tiny string made of so many wonderful tiny rocks. King Spring held it out for Diggie to take.

"Oh!" he exclaimed. "Is that for me?"

"It could be," replied King Spring, "but first, there is something you could do for me."

"Oh yes, and what might that be?" asked Diggie suspiciously.

"Well," said King Spring, "if you could call in and see us all on your return trip. I would like you to take one of the younger springs with you back to your solar system, as we could do with some more new oil."

"No problem," said Diggie. "Anything for a friend of Mr Whisky-bee."

After all their goodbyes, Diggie presented them with their little silver and gold bell. Then the little spaceship rose high into the clouds and onwards to Earth, the next planet and the one Diggie was so keen to see.

18. EARTH, THE FACTS

Both Diggie and Mr Whisky-bee were very excited as this was the planet where the first signal had come from.

"Where will we land?" asked Mr Whisky-bee.

"We will have to be very careful. There's a lot of wet stuff called water that covers the Earth," replied Diggie, "and I am unsure if it's the same consistency as the water on our planet back home. But let's find out some more!"

Diggie asked Mr Whisky-bee to pass him his book, and Diggie read out loud all about countries and continents.

Earth

Diameter: 12,756.3 km.

Earth is the 3rd planet from the Sun and the 5th largest. It is the densest planet in the solar system.

The Earth is divided into several layers. The layers vary considerably in thickness. They are thinner under the oceans and thicker under the continents.

The inner core (in the middle) and the crust (on the outside) are solid. The layers in between, the outer core and the mantle, are plastic or semi-fluid.

The core is probably made mostly of iron or nickel iron. Temperatures at the centre of the core may be as high as 7500k – that's hotter than the surface of the Sun.

Mr Whisky-bee was looking through the window.

"What do you think of that space there to land?" asked Diggie.

"What do I think of what?" asked Mr Whisky-bee. "You lost me when you mentioned continents."

"Oh, Mr Whisky-bee!" exclaimed Diggie. "Never mind. Buckle up. We're about to land!"

Diggie was still homing in on the original signal. "There!" he cried.

They looked down and saw a small housing estate.

19. HUMANS

"You can't land there," cried Mr Whisky-bee. "There are too many square things!"

"Those are houses. That's where people live. There's not much room, but I think we can make it."

The spaceship hovered over a small back garden and Diggie slowly and carefully brought his little spaceship I-I into land. It was very dark outside, and Diggie knew that meant the Sun was round the other side of the planet.

"We must hide the spaceship," said Mr Whisky-bee.

"Why?" asked Diggie.

"My family have been here before from my home planet, and they told me that the creatures that live here panic whenever they see something they don't understand," Mr Whisky-bee explained.

"Oh dear, why didn't you tell me before?"

"Well, it's only now when I saw all those square houses that I remembered seeing some pictures my mum showed me when I was young."

Diggie looked worried. "I don't know how to hide my spaceship."

"That's ok, I do," said Mr Whisky-bee. And with that, he left the ship. Outside, he began to spin just like a tornado, weaving a fine web that covered the whole ship, including the trailer. Once covered, they became invisible.

"How wonderful!" said Diggie. "I have known you for so many years, but I never knew you could do that."

Diggie looked at his calendar. He had made good time, and there were still two weeks to go before the start of the new millennium.

The next morning, Diggie and Mr Whisky-bee were woken by a noise outside. Just as they looked out, they saw a vehicle pulling away from the house.

"What was that?" asked Mr Whisky-bee.

"I don't know," replied Diggie.

"Let's go exploring!" said Mr Whisky-bee, and before Diggie could reply, he had gone. Diggie rushed after him, just in time to see Mr Whisky-bee disappearing into the back of the house.

Oh dear! thought Diggie, and quickly followed him.

Inside the house, two children were arguing.

"That's mine," shouted one child, snatching a square box from the larger child. As he swung round with it in his hand, there was a loud bang as it hit Diggie's space helmet. The smaller child stood frozen to the spot.

Mr Whisky-bee, who was a little afraid of all the shouting, hid behind Diggie.

The smallest of the children was called Carlie, and he was shouting at the larger child, his sister Tara. Tara shouted back, "That's not funny! Tell Mark to go home. This is a private argument, and look at the damage on my lunch box. Mum's going to be so cross."

Carlie was almost nine and Mark, his best friend who lived next door, was eleven.

"That's not Mark," replied Carlie.

Tara, who was fourteen, was supposed to be taking care of Carlie during the holidays while their parents were at work.

"Don't be daft!" she shouted. "It's just like Mark, dressing up as an alien and trying to scare me. I'm not falling for it!"

"That's not Mark!" insisted Carlie, as he stamped his foot on the ground.

"Well, who is it then?" Tara stepped forward and pulled Diggie's helmet straight off.

Not quite sure what she had exposed, she poked Diggie in the face.

"That tickles!" he said, and smiled.

Tara screamed, bolted from the room, and ran up the stairs. She kept right on screaming, without even stopping to draw breath, until she reached her bedroom.

Carlie, though, was much braver. "Where on earth did you come from?"

"Well, not exactly Earth," replied Diggie.

Now upstairs, poor Tara was thinking the worst. *What if this alien was here to steal her brother? What if she'd waited too long and he already had?* She had to go back downstairs and save him.

So, she bravely crept back down, one step at a time. On the bottom stair she could see into the kitchen where Carlie was having a conversation with the alien. *I must be dreaming!* she thought.

"Did I upset your sister?" asked Diggie.

"Oh no, she just doesn't believe in people from other planets," replied Carlie.

"Well, we don't want to upset her any more now, do we?" said Diggie, as he looked over Carlie's shoulder and saw Tara peeping round the doorway. "We had better go."

"What do you mean 'we'?" asked Carlie. "How many of you are there? Is this an invasion?"

"No," laughed Diggie, "just me and Mr Whisky-bee."

On hearing his name, Mr Whisky-bee floated out from behind Diggie. But this proved too much for Tara. She took one look at Mr Whisky-bee, and fainted flat on the floor.

Diggie hurried round trying to help, while Mr Whisky-bee had gone all shy again and was hiding behind a chair.

"Oh, she'll be alright," said Carlie, as though this was something that happened every day.

Finally, she came round and was helped to sit down. But all the time, Tara never took her eyes off Mr Whisky-bee.

"He is a little strange, but completely harmless, you know," Diggie assured her.

Tara was not convinced, but sat and said nothing while Diggie explained how he had followed a radio signal from their house, talking all about the Millennium, all the way from his home planet. And that's how he had come to land in their garden.

"That'll be my dad," said Carlie. "He's always playing with his radio equipment. But you're a little late for the Millennium, you know."

"Oh dear, oh dear. I don't know how that happened. I was so looking forward to it," replied Diggie.

"Oh!" said Carlie, "Not to worry. I promise, you didn't miss much, as I remember Dad telling me all about it. He was so disappointed himself. Because there was so much cloud in the sky, he couldn't see anything through his telescope."

After a little pause, Diggie asked, "Can we stay in your garden for a little while?"

"Ok," said Carlie. "You can borrow my tent."

"What's a tent?" Mr Whisky-bee asked bravely.

"Somewhere you can sleep."

"That's very kind, but will there be room for a tent as well as our spaceship?" asked Diggie. "It does take up rather a lot of room out there."

Tara's curiosity finally got the better of her. She could hardly believe her ears, so she just had to see for herself. Slowly, she stepped towards the back door, but Carlie was ahead of her. They peered into the garden but saw nothing.

"This has got to be a joke!" snapped Tara.

"Oh no," said Mr whisky-bee. "I covered it up with my invisible net. Would you like to see?"

So they all went outside and when Mr Whisky-bee lifted the net, there was the spaceship, complete with trailer.

"Quick," said Tara, "cover it back up. If anyone sees it, they'll tow it away!"

Mr Whisky-bee obliged.

"What will we tell Mum and Dad?" asked Tara.

"Nothing," said Carlie. "It's our secret. Mum and Dad never come into the garden at this time of year, and if we take out the rubbish when asked, they hardly ever need to step outside."

"Ok then, it's our secret," said Tara.

They all went back inside and Tara, who was not quite sure what to do next, asked, "Anyone for tea?" It was always something her mother said when she was lost for words.

It turned out that Diggie and Mr Whisky-bee had landed slap-bang in the middle of a housing estate, just outside a town called Brigg, in the north east of England. It was better known as the Tea Town, because everyone came from miles around to buy tea from a little shop that sold almost every brand and colour of tea.

Diggie had no idea what tea was, but agreed, as it seemed to make Tara happy to be doing something. He thought it would take her mind off the recent shock.

"Good idea!" shouted Carlie, but his eyes were still fixed on the garden. *Mmm, time to explore later,* he thought. He was so looking forward to seeing inside the spaceship, but now he just wanted to humour Tara until she calmed down enough to accept that there were actually two spacemen in their kitchen.

As they chatted away, time flew by. Tara was explaining all about Christmas to Mr Whisky-bee, but he just didn't understand, so she gave him a book to read, all about giving of gifts and the three wise men, who were kings bringing gifts for a baby called Jesus. Diggie had heard of Christmas before, so he told Mr Whisky-bee not to worry, he would explain it all to him later.

They were so busy chatting that no-one noticed it was almost 5:30, when Carlie and Tara's mum was due home from work. Then suddenly, they heard a key turning in the front door.

"What was that?" asked Mr Whisky-bee. The children looked up at the kitchen clock, then stared at each other and said jointly, "Mum!"

Now, Diggie had seen Mr Whisky-bee move quickly, but these two earthlings were rushing around in pure panic.

"Quick!" said Tara. "Go into the hall and stall Mum. I'll hide Diggie and Mr Whisky-bee."

"Why?" asked Mr Whisky-bee, as Carlie dashed into the hall, just in time to stop his mother from reaching the kitchen.

"Why hide?" Mr Whisky-bee asked again.

"Just for a little while, until we've had time to explain to Mum and Dad," said Tara. "Remember what happened to me! I don't want that to happen to my mum – she may never get over the shock!"

"Come on, Mr Whisky-bee!" said Diggie. "We can hide out in the spaceship."

Mr Whisky-bee was still talking to himself as Diggie ushered him outside.

"Now, what's all this?" asked Carlie's mother suspiciously. "You'd like to carry my shopping into the kitchen, put it away, and make me a nice cup of tea?"

Just then, Tara joined them. "Yes, that's right, Mum," said Tara. "You go and put your feet up, and I'll make tea."

"Well, if you're sure. I could do with some rest! It has been such a busy day at work today."

The children took the bags into the kitchen and set to work making tea. Soon afterwards, their father arrived home and, after saying hello to the children, he went to join their mother in the living room. "What's up with the kids?" he asked.

"I'm not sure! I can only think it's to do with Christmas, and they're making an extra effort to be good," replied their mother. "That's going to be worth seeing!"

They burst out laughing together, as they settled down beside the fire.

Meanwhile, back in the kitchen, Carlie and Tara couldn't make up their minds. "Let's tell them after tea," said Carlie.

"No, it's too soon," said Tara.

"Well, when?" asked Carlie. "There'll never be a right time to tell them, and it will be impossible to keep it a secret forever."

"Ok, I know," said Tara. "We can tell them tonight. When Dad comes up and says goodnight, we can tell him then. After all, it was his signal that Diggie tracked here, and then he can tell Mum. He knows how to handle her so that she won't get over-excited."

"Like you did!" said Carlie, laughing.

As they all sat down for tea, Carlie was finding it very difficult not to say anything, but Tara kept giving him a hard stare.

"What's up with you two?" asked Dad.

"Nothing," said Tara quickly, before Carlie had a chance to open his mouth. "Nothing at all! Just excited about Christmas."

After tea, they all went into the living room to watch some TV. Halfway through the film, they all heard a strange noise coming from the kitchen.

"What's that?" asked Mum. "Sounds like someone's in the kitchen!"

Tara and Carlie jumped up together. "That's Ok, Mum. We'll check it out!"

They arrived in the kitchen just as the back door was closing. They dashed over to it, and were just about to go outside when their father entered. "Well, you two, what was it?" he asked.

"Oh, just a stray cat," answered Tara, thinking quickly. "Carlie must have left the door open a little when he took the rubbish out." That explanation seemed to satisfy their dad. "Well, kids, time for bed! Up you go, and I'll be along shortly to say goodnight."

Once they were in their pyjamas and had brushed their teeth, Tara went into her brother's room and perched on the side of his bed.

"So, what are we going to do?" asked Carlie.

"I don't know," replied Tara. "Do we tell Dad tonight, or when?"

Just then, Dad appeared in the doorway. "Tell Dad what?" he asked.

Tara looked at Carlie and thought, *It's now or never*! She was just about to spill the beans, when Carlie reached out and pinched her.

She jumped. "What was that for? We agreed!"

"Oh, Ok," said Carlie, "but let me tell him."

"Right, kids, let's have it! What's going on?"

"Well, Dad, it's like this," Carlie began, then he explained all about what had happened that day.

His father listened patiently while Carlie told him the whole story. Then, without saying a word, he got up and looked out of the window.

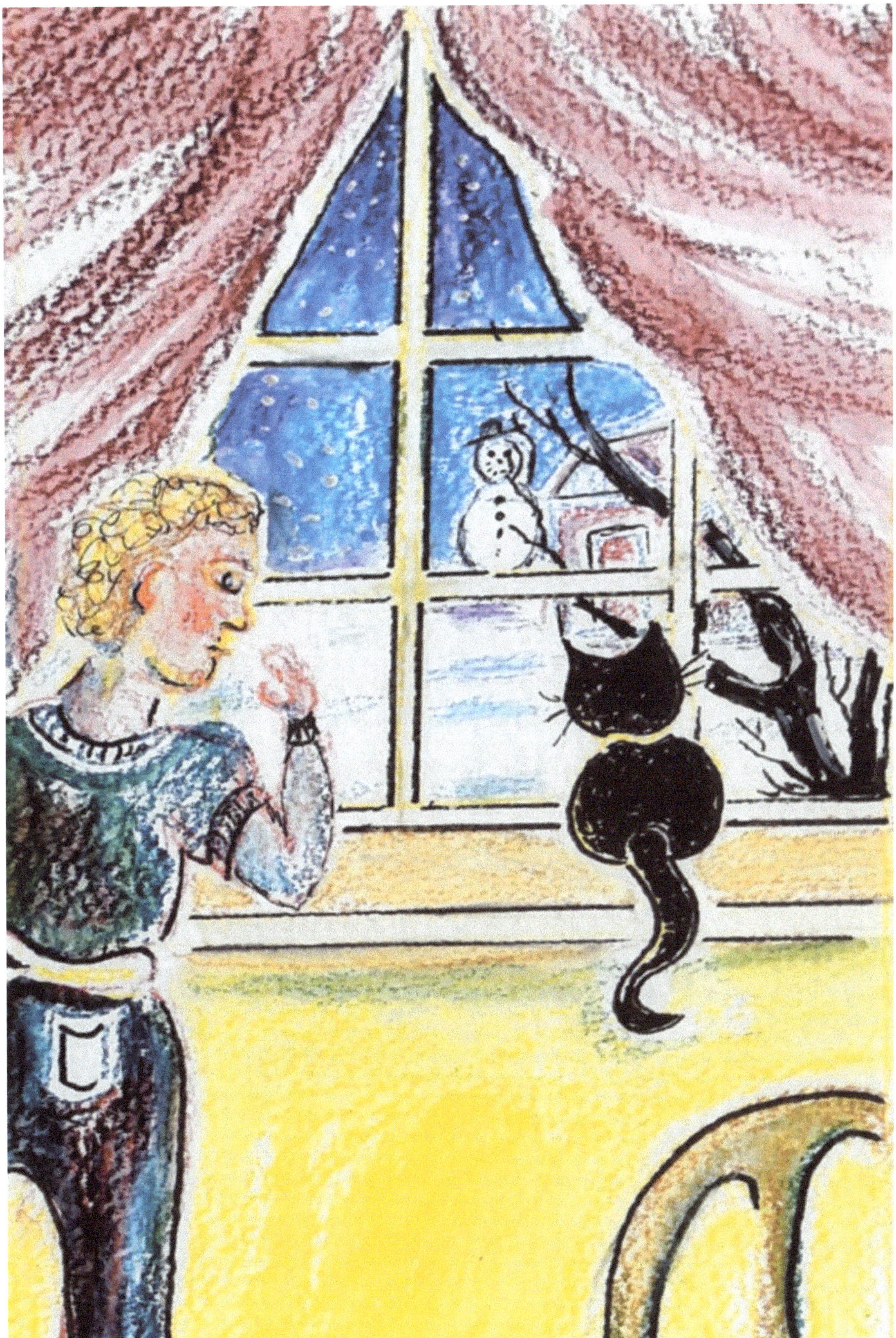

"So, down there, under an invisible net, is a spaceship and two spacemen! Hmm." He repeated the words, as if he was trying to convince himself of what he was saying. But he knew that if anyone was going to get a good night's sleep, he would need to humour his children.

"Ok, kids. Well, it's too late and too dark now to pay them a visit, so get some sleep and we'll go and say good morning to them after we've all had a good night's rest."

The following morning Mum got up first and was making breakfast when she was joined by the rest of the family, whispering amongst themselves.

"What are you all whispering about?" she asked.

"Nothing, Mum," said Tara.

"Well, almost," Carlie laughed, as they made their way to the back door.

Outside, everyone felt about in earnest but there was nothing there.

Dad smiled. "Well, kids, you had me going for a minute." He walked back inside and, shortly after, Tara and Carlie came in.

"I don't understand," said Carlie. "Diggie and Mr Whisky-bee would never have left without saying goodbye."

"What was that name again?" asked Mum.

"Diggie," replied Carlie.

Mum walked over to the fridge, where a note on a small scrap of paper was stuck under one of the fridge magnets.

It read: "Gone to see Venus and Mercury. Will pop in on return visit. Diggie & Mr Whisky-bee."

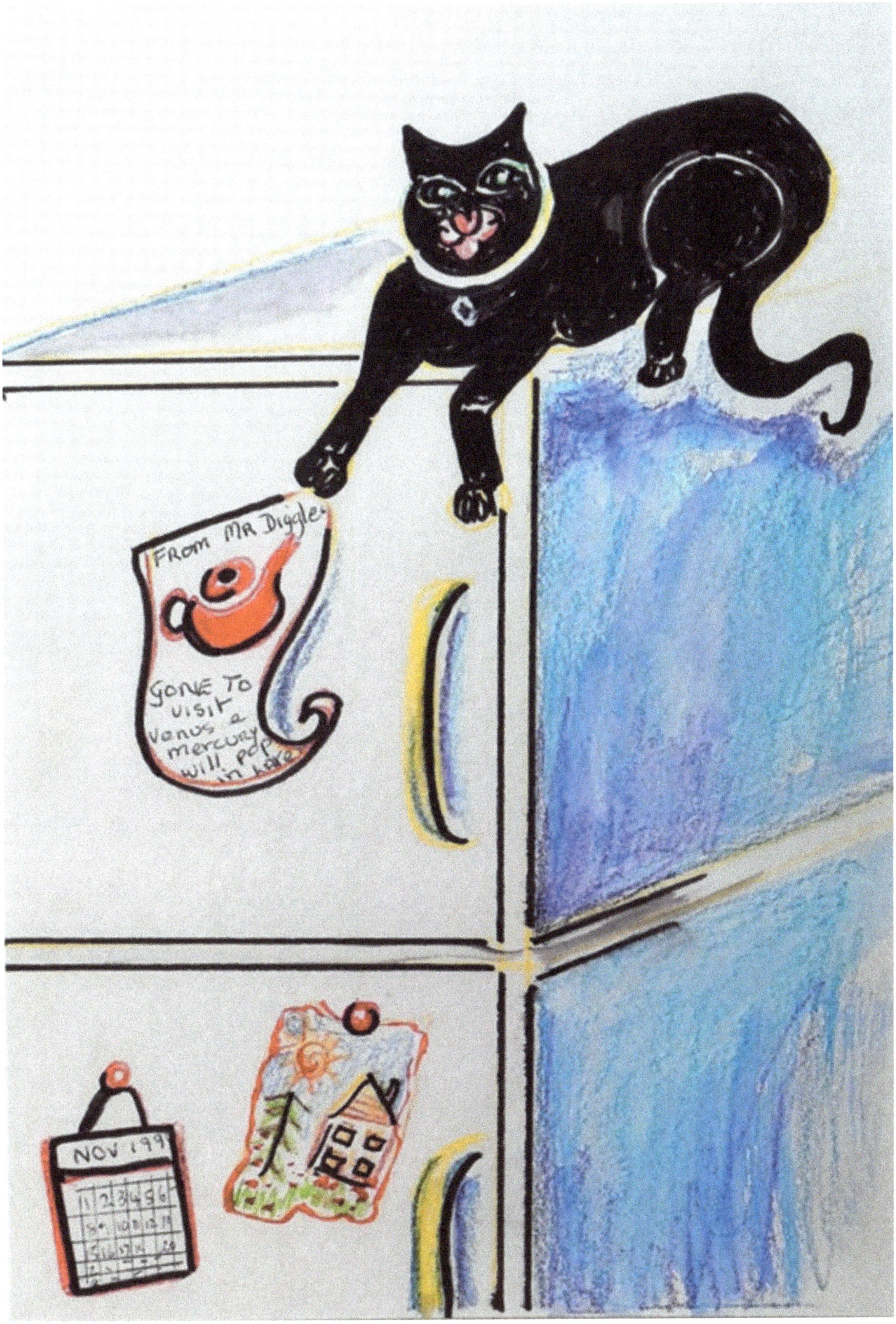

Meanwhile, high among the stars, Mr Whisky-bee was reading aloud from the book Tara had given him, which explained all about Christmas.

"It's all about a special baby being born called Jesus, and the gifts people gave each other," he explained.

"How exciting," said Diggie. "Presents for all good boys and girls."

Just then, his attention was drawn to the planet coming into view. "Never mind Christmas for now, Mr Whisky-bee. Pass me the planet book, please!"

"Can I read it?" asked Mr Whisky-bee.

"Of course you can!" said Diggie.

But after reading out a passage to Diggie, Mr Whisky-bee began to shake. "It sounds very scary down there."

20. VENUS, THE FACTS

Venus

Diameter: 12,103.6 km.

Venus is the 2nd planet from the Sun and the 6th largest.

There are strong winds as you approach, but they become milder the closer you get. Venus probably once had large amounts of water, like Earth, but at some time in the past it all boiled away, and Venus is now very dry.

There are no small craters on Venus. It seems meteoroids burned up in Venus's dense atmosphere before reaching the surface.

Venus has no magnetic field, perhaps because it turns round and round very slowly.

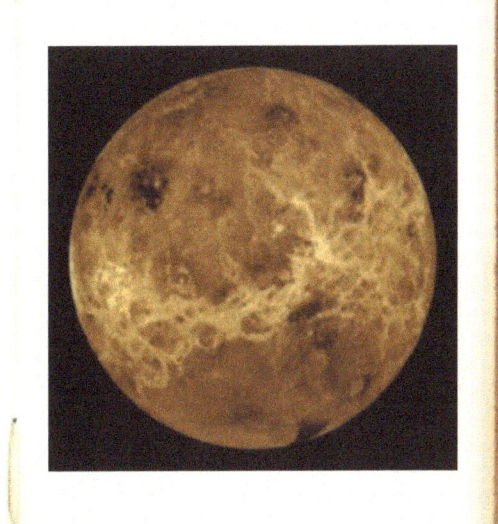

"Are we going to be safe?" asked Mr Whisky-bee.
"Of course! This little spaceship can handle it," said Diggie.
Mr Whisky-bee had never heard anyone talk about Venus on his home planet, so neither of them knew what they would find there.

21. JELLY WALLS

They landed with a gentle bump and left the spaceship I-I to explore. With such a big planet and so much to see, Mr Whisky-bee didn't know which way to go first. He spun round in circles; he seemed just a little more afraid than normal.

Diggie laughed as he told him, "Now, Mr Whisky-bee, the very best place to start exploring is always under your nose."

Mr Whisky-bee looked under his nose and replied, "But I know what's under my nose. It's my cloud."

"No, Mr Whisky-bee, you don't understand. I mean… Oh well, never mind – let's start here!"

As Diggie reached down and touched the ground, his hand disappeared in front of his very eyes. He quickly pulled it back and looked at it in disbelief. Once again, he reached down, and the same thing happened.

"Look!" screamed Mr Whisky-bee. He pointed towards what was left of the spaceship, just before it disappeared under the surface.

"Oh, my goodness!" exclaimed Diggie. "What will we do now?" Just then the ground under their feet softened, and they gradually began to be eaten up by the very ground they stood on. Mr Whisky-bee was hiding in his own cloud – that was just another one of the magical things he could do, and he always did it when he was afraid.

Diggie could remember whenever Mr Whisky-bee saw a tiny little animal called a cowwie on their own planet, he would hide – even though a cowwie was just like the mouse you would see on earth. Cowwies were small and covered in multicoloured fur, but every time they coughed and sneezed, their hair would grow an inch, so it didn't take long for them to have to go and get a haircut. Afterwards, they always looked so strange, because their skin was multicoloured, just like their hair. Back on Diggie's home planet, the hair was used to make a special fuel that helped to fly Diggie's spaceship, and to power all sorts of things.

Suddenly… Plop! Mr Whisky-bee and Diggie fell into a large cavern, and plop was exactly the sound they made as they landed on a wobbly, jelly-like surface. It wasn't long before they were joined by a creature that looked like a huge redcurrant jelly.

"I wonder if it tastes sweet, like fruit," whispered Mr Whisky-bee.

"Shh! Shh!" said Diggie. "He might be able to hear us."

"Well, not exactly hear," replied the creature, "but I do understand what you are saying by reading your thoughts," said the big jelly blob in front of them.

Diggie exclaimed, "You're telepathic!"

Mr Whisky-bee, pulling at Diggie's arm, said, "What's telepathic?"

But Diggie was too busy talking to the alien to answer. "Maybe you would be so good as to tell me, why you have sucked my spaceship I-I and us down into this cavern? Lovely as it is, I would much rather be above ground."

"Oh, I'm so sorry! I didn't know. You see, we prefer it down here," answered the wibbly wobbly structure in front of Diggie, and it began to smile.

The cavern began to fill with new Wibbly Wobbly creatures, all interested in seeing the aliens who had just landed on their planet. Mr Whisky-bee was now feeling more confident and began whizzing around examining this new Wibbly Wobbly world.

Just then, something caught his eye. It was a baby Wibbly Wobbly. Mr Whisky-bee flew over to take a closer look, but was so busy looking at the baby that he forgot to watch where he was going. He flew straight into the jelly wall, only to bounce off and ricochet around the cavern like a bullet.

Diggie looked up in alarm.

"Oh, not to worry," said the big Wibbly Wobble. "He should stop in a few minutes or so."

Diggie watched as Mr Whisky-bee flew around, bouncing from one jelly wall to another. It did look quite funny, and Diggie began to laugh, as did all the Wibbly Wobblies. As they laughed, they wibbled and wobbled even more, making Diggie laugh so much he almost cried.

Later, after everyone had calmed down and Mr Whisky-bee had stopped bouncing, the big Wibbly Wobbly asked what had made them come to his planet. Diggie explained that he was collecting rocks, but the big Wibbly Wobbly asked, "What's a rock?"

Diggie looked around and realised that he couldn't see any hard rocks, only jelly.

Diggie had never come across this before. "Well, a rock is a bit of a planet," he answered.

The big Wibbly Wobbly reached out, tore a piece out of the wall, and held it out for Diggie to take.

This must be the strangest rock of all, Diggie thought, as he reached out his hand to accept it. The big Wibbly Wobbly plopped it into his palm and it lay there shaking, just like a jelly.

Delighted with this unusual new addition to his collection, Diggie then gave the big Wibbly Wobbly the little bell as a gift.

As they both smiled and thanked each other, neither knew exactly what they were supposed to do with the strange gifts.

The big Wibbly Wobbly showed Diggie to the exit of the cavern and watched as he and Mr Whisky-bee took off towards the next and last planet, Mercury.

22. MERCURY, THE FACTS

Diggie and Mr Whisky-bee consulted the red book to see what they could find out about Mercury. It read:

Mercury

Diameter: 4,880 km.

Mercury is the closest planet to the Sun and the 8th largest.

The temperature varies enormously on Mercury, the most extreme planet in the solar system. A large iron core, with a radius of 1800-1900 km, dominates Mercury's interior. The silicate outer shell is only 500-600 km thick. At least some of the core is probably molten.

Mercury has a small magnetic field whose strength is about 1% of that of Earth's.

Mercury also has a region of relatively smooth plains. Some may be the result of ancient volcanic activity, but some may be the result of the deposition of ejects from crater impacts.

Mr Whisky-bee looked at Diggie and admitted that he hadn't understood much of what the book had to say.

"Never mind, Mr Whisky-bee," replied Diggie. "One day, I'll explain."

23. TEAPOT

Now, because Mercury was so close to the Sun, they couldn't stop there for long and decided to make a quick landing to collect a piece of rock. Diggie had to put on a special spacesuit made from an unusual gold metal that could only be found on his friend Mog's planet, to help him shield from the heat. But Mr Whisky-bee would have to stay on the spaceship.

Diggie quickly found a small piece of rock, and returned to the spaceship, then prepared to fly off again. You see, no-one lives on Mercury, because it's much too hot! Or so they thought.

Back on the spaceship, Diggie removed his spacesuit then he held out his hand to show the new rock to Mr Whisky-bee. But the rock began to move in his hand, until it seemed to morph into a shape that looked just like a teapot. It was red and orange, just like the colour of a flame, but it wasn't hot like a flame.

Once it had fully formed, it asked, "Where are we going?"

Mr Whisky-bee and Diggie were speechless, then the little flame spoke again. "I like your spaceship. Are we going far?"

It was Diggie who spoke first. He didn't know what to call the little flame, but he decided it reminded him of the teapot he had seen Tara making tea with, so he asked Teapot if he needed to return to his own planet.

"Oh no, I like it here on your spaceship, but I would like to know where we are going."

"We are first returning to Earth, on our way back to our own world," Diggie explained.

"Oh, how wonderful. I would love to come with you."

Diggie realised they had no choice, as it was too late to return to Mercury. So onwards to Earth they all went.

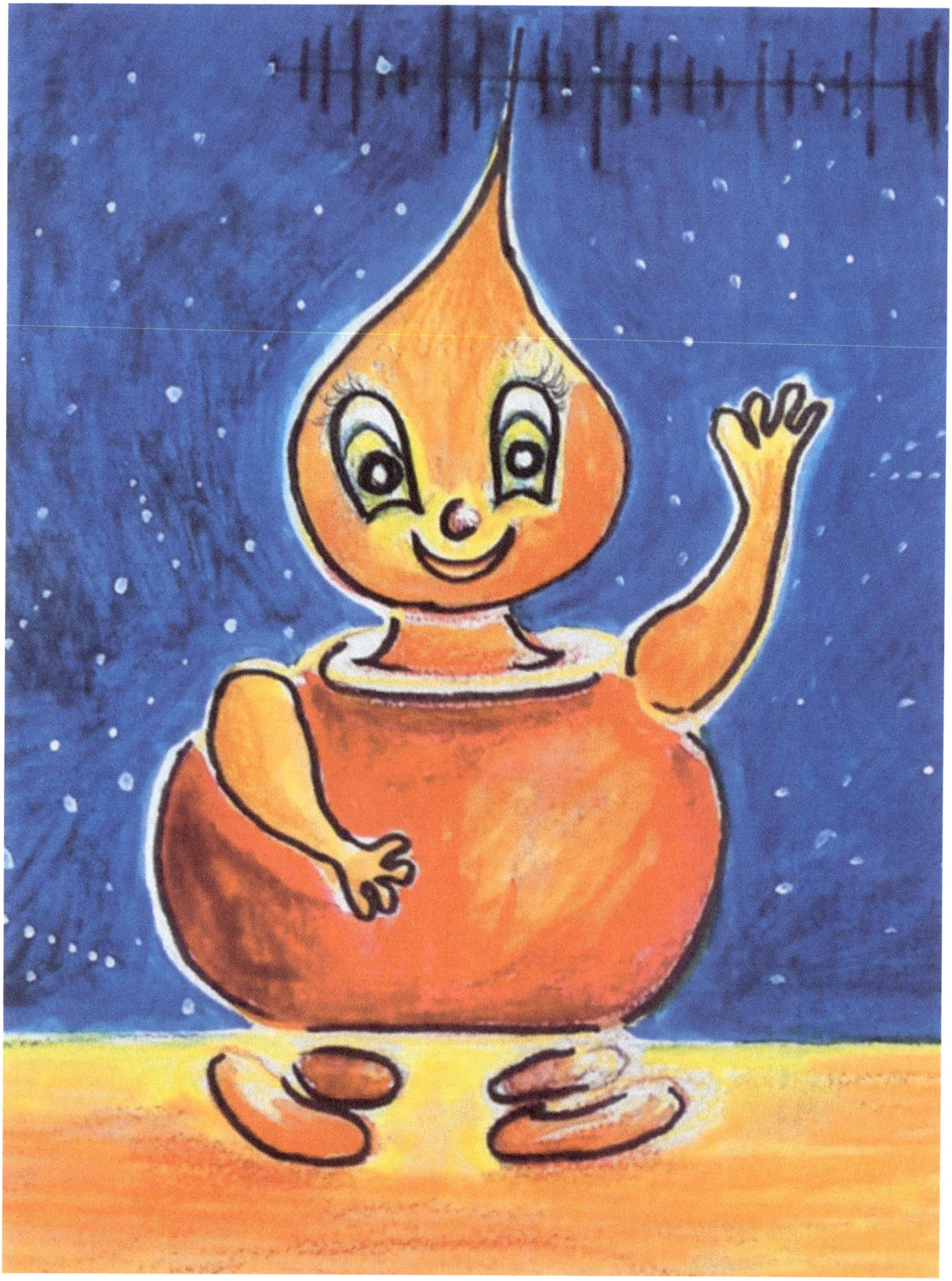

24. THE SUN, THE FACTS

The last pages in the book were all about the Sun. They read:

Sun

Diameter: 1,390,000 km.

The Sun is an ordinary G2 star, one of more than 100 billion stars in this galaxy. The Sun is by far the largest object in the solar system.

The outer layers of the Sun exhibit differential rotation. At the Equator, the surface rotates once every 25.4 days, whereas near the Poles it takes as much as 36 days to complete a rotation. This odd behaviour is due to the fact that the Sun is not a solid body like the Earth.

The Sun's magnetic field is very strong and very complicated.

The solar wind has large effects on the tails of comets and even has measurable effects on the trajectories of spacecraft.

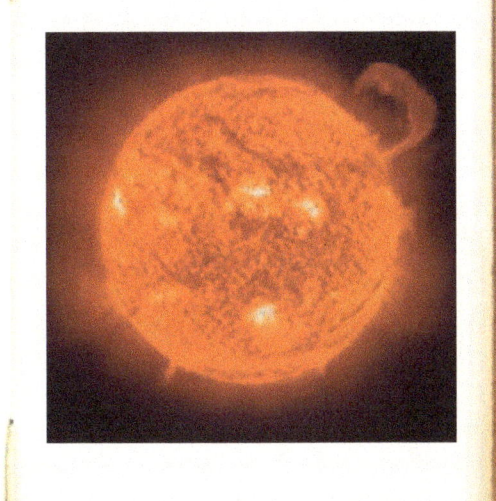

Diggie had read about the solar winds before, as he had often used them back in his own solar system, with a similar sun. He was hoping to use them to get back to Earth to help save some fuel.

25. TEACUP

Diggie checked his maps. As he did so, he pulled a lever down beside his seat and, to Mr Whisky-bee's amazement, the engines stopped, and huge wings appeared on each side of the spaceship.

"Oh!" exclaimed Mr Whisky-bee at the wonder of it.

Meanwhile, back on Earth, it was Christmas Eve. Tara and Carlie were getting ready for the following day, wrapping gifts and playing games.

It was getting late when Dad arrived home from work that night, so Tara and Carlie were all ready for bed. After their father had eaten his tea, he saw Carlie staring out of the window towards the sky, but there were no stars to be seen that evening, only soft snowflakes drifting gracefully to earth.

Dad put his arm around Carlie's shoulder and said, "Never mind! I'm sure your new friends will come back one day."

Carlie shrugged his shoulders and turned to say goodnight to his parents, then he and Tara went off to bed with the saddest of faces. The children had begun to think Diggie and Mr Whisky-bee had just been a strange daydream and that they would never see them again.

Right at that moment, way above the house tops and heading for Earth, were Diggie and Mr Whisky bee.

Whoosh! The little spaceship was taken completely by surprise, and Diggie quickly pulled the lever that retracted the sails then re-engaged the engine.

"Must be one of those rocket things this planet keeps sending up," said Mr Whisky-bee.

Then it happened again. Whoosh!

"And since when have rockets flown sideways?" asked Diggie, confused.

There it was again: whoosh! And this time it was heading straight for them!

Diggie brought his ship to a halt, and a red light on the other craft came closer and closer till it was nose-to-nose with Diggie's spaceship.

"What is it?" asked Mr Whisky-bee, looking anxious.

"I'm not sure," replied Diggie.

He clicked open his cockpit. "Hello there," he shouted across to the other craft.

"Ho! Ho! Ho!" came back the reply.

"It's Father Christmas," said Mr Whisky-bee, remembering the stories from the book Tara had given him.

"Where are you going so late on Christmas Eve?" asked Father Christmas.

Diggie explained that they were on their way to see Carlie and Tara.

"Hmm, just been there. They're fast asleep now, so don't disturb them until morning," said Father Christmas.

No sooner had he said 'morning' than 'Whoosh!' he was gone again.

Mr Whisky-bee asked Diggie more about Christmas. That's when Diggie remembered all about the box he had been given by the Stacker people, which was still wrapped up under his seat. "I still need to open the present from the Stacker people," he said. "But what will we do about the children? We must give them a present."

"Not to worry," replied Mr Whisky-bee. "Remember, when we first arrived, they both seemed to want what Tara was calling a pack up box?"

"Yes," said Diggie.

"Do you remember when it hit your helmet?" giggled Mr Whisky-bee.

"Yes, yes," said Diggie a little impatiently. He felt rather guilty at being a little to blame for the box's damage.

"Well I could make them both a new lunch box," said Mr Whisky-bee.

Just then the little teapot poked his head up from where he had been sleeping. "I just heard you talking about the box under your seat. Did you know it keeps making strange noises?" he asked.

Mr Whisky-bee looked at Diggie, and together they said, "Noises?"

"Yes," said Teapot.

Slowly and carefully, Diggie retrieved the packet from under his seat then gently pulled the little bow. Before he could remove any more wrapping, up popped the lid, and there was a stowaway! "About time," said the little Stacker. "I thought you were never going to let me out."

"Let you out? We never knew you were in there at all," said an astonished Diggie.

"Well, no harm done," said the little Stacker. "Now what about presents for the children? Can I have a present? I like presents. My family love to give presents all year round."

Diggie and Mr Whisky-bee were still in a state of shock at finding the little stowaway.

"Not so fast,'" said Diggie. "Do the Stackers know you stowed away in the box?"

"Of course. I promised them I would get you to drop me off on your way home."

A likely story, thought Diggie. But it was too late now to sort out the little Stacker.

26. GIFTS

"What about presents for the children?" the little Stacker asked. "I like the idea of new lunch boxes, but what are lunch boxes?"

As Diggie tried to explain what a lunch box was, Mr Whisky-bee asked, "What's your name little one?"

"I don't know how to say it in your language," came the answer.

At that point, Teapot said, "Well, you said I looked just like a teapot because I was so small and reminded you of a teapot, whatever that is. So let's call this little Stacker something smaller than me."

Diggie gave it a little thought, then asked the little Stacker what he thought about the name Teacup.

"Sounds good to me, but I have no idea what a teacup is. Not to worry. I like it, so everybody can call me Teacup."

Diggie was still giving the idea of lunch boxes some thought, but just couldn't think of anything else. Eventually, he told Mr Whisky-bee, "Lunch boxes sounds like a good idea to me too, so lunch boxes it is. Do you think you really could make them, Mr Whisky-bee?"

"Well, it won't be exactly the same as the one that hit your helmet, but maybe they won't mind a different shape altogether."

"What are you thinking, Mr Whisky-bee?" asked Diggie.

"The original box wasn't really a good design – it broke very easily," he replied. "If I make the new boxes round, like your helmet, they should be much stronger. And if I add a shoulder strap, they should be easy to carry."

"But how will the box stand up?" asked Diggie.

"Let me show you," said Mr Whisky-bee, as he went into one of his spins. After a little while, from under Mr Whisky-bee's cloud, out popped a lunch box with little round feet.

"That's super, but it's a bit plain. Can you colour it, and make the one for Carlie look like Jupiter and the one for Tara a nice red one to look like Mars? Then they'll be able to tell whose is whose straight away."

"Oh, you are clever, Diggie!" said Mr Whisky-bee.

It didn't take long for Mr Whisky-bee to finish both containers, and what a good job he had done! Each one had little ball-shaped legs, a little lid that opened when you pressed a heart-shaped button just below the opening, and a smart strap to carry it with.

"Do you think that the children will like them?" asked Mr Whisky-bee.

"Oh, I'm sure they will, Mr Whisky-bee," said Diggie.

The spaceship was already hovering gently over the garden, and slowly down they all went.

Remembering what Father Christmas had said, they settled down to sleep. After all, they had been on a very long trip and were very tired.

The next morning, the only thing on Tara and Carlie's minds was presents. Their mum was already up and making breakfast in the kitchen when they came bounding downstairs. When she heard the sound of children rustling paper in the living room, she went in to wish them a Merry Christmas.

"Only one present now," she reminded them. "Save some till Dad gets up!"

Knock, knock!

"Now, who can that be at this time of the morning?" Mum wondered aloud. "Tara, do go and see, and I'll go and give Dad a call."

Tara opened the back door to find Mark from next door, along with his two brothers, Oliver and Harry, and his sister, Hannah.

"Come in quickly," shivered Tara. "It's so cold out there this morning."

They all entered the living room just as Dad arrived, still wearing his pyjamas and dressing gown. Everyone was very excited. The children were running everywhere, playing with their new toys and making such a racket that nobody could have heard a trumpet sound, let alone another knock at the door.

Then there it was: Knock, knock!

Dad said to Mum, "Did you hear anything, darling?"

"No, I don't think so," she replied.

"I'll just go and check," said Dad.

The knocking on the door grew louder as he entered the kitchen. And when he opened the door, he was greeted by Diggie, who was in a hurry to get inside out of the cold.

Gently pushing his way into the kitchen, Diggie said, "Very cold out there today, sir!"

Dad stood still, staring at Diggie, not knowing who or what he had just opened the door to. Diggie introduced himself, and then Mr Whisky-bee.

Mum came into the kitchen just as the kettle was boiling. Diggie introduced himself again. "I'm Diggie," he announced.

Mr Whisky-bee had noticed the kettle boiling and remembered that Tara had made tea before when someone had a shock.

"Tea anyone?" he asked, as he lifted the kettle purely by thought.

Mum and Dad were speechless, frozen to the spot.

Just then Carlie entered the kitchen. "Diggie!" He screamed so loudly that all the other children came running out of the living room and into the kitchen.

Tara rushed up and threw her arms around Diggie as if she had known him all her life. She squeezed so tightly that it took his breath away.

By now Mum had collapsed into the kitchen chair, while Dad was still frozen to the same spot, beside the open back door.

"Close the door – it's so cold in here!" complained little Harry. He was only six years old and didn't see anything strange about a spaceman standing beside him while another made tea.

His sister Hannah and brothers, Oliver and Mark, were older. Hannah was eight, while Oliver was almost ten and Mark eleven; they just didn't know what to make of it all.

"I guess if Tara and Carlie hadn't been so friendly with Diggie and Mr Whisky-bee, we would have been just a little afraid," Mark admitted later.

Mr Whisky-bee had successfully made the tea and was handing Mum a cuppa.

Tara said, "Let's all go into the living room so I can give Diggie a present I got for him."

The children suddenly remembered the presents around the tree. And without giving a second thought to the fact that they had just met two spacemen, they all dashed back into the living room, followed by Diggie and Mr Whisky-bee.

Dad was still numb when Mum, who was still sitting down, finally said, "What? Who was that, dear?"

Although Dad was a scientist, he didn't know how to answer without sounding a little scary, so he said, "It's ok, darling! It's just the children's new friends, Diggie and Mr Whisky-bee."

As he spoke, he was trying to convince himself that there was nothing unusual about the children's new friends being aliens. He walked over and helped his wife to stand. "Let's go and see what the kids are doing," he said.

As they entered the room, Mum was still feeling a little shaky. And seeing two spacemen in her living room, she promptly collapsed into the big armchair. Dad edged slowly towards the fireplace, as if he was trying not to draw any attention to himself.

Tara and Carlie gave Diggie his gift. He slowly opened the paper to find the most magnificent piece of jet-black rock.

"It's only coal," said Carlie, "and I'm not even sure you can call it rock."

But Diggie smiled with delight. "It's fantastic! Carlie, Tara, thank you so much. I don't think I have got anything like it in my collection."

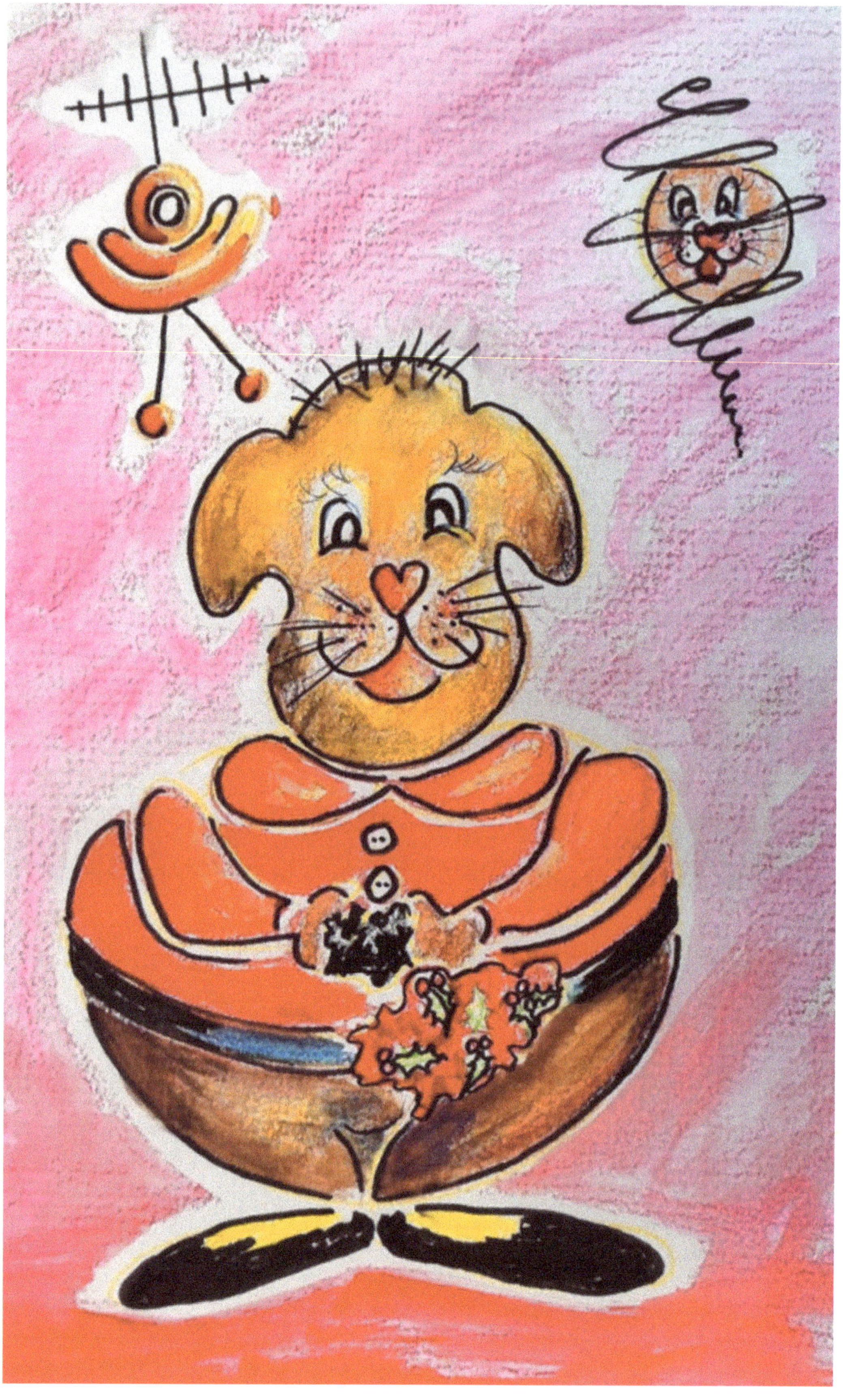

Then came a little noise. "Have I got a present?" asked Mr Whisky-bee hopefully.

"Of course!" said Tara, as she handed Mr Whisky-bee a packet.

He opened it and chuckled with glee. "Oh, it's me and Diggie." Tara had always been very good at drawing and painting, so she had drawn a picture of them both. Mr Whisky-bee was delighted with it, and all the children gathered round to see.

"It's very good," said Mark. "It looks just like them. Have you met them before?"

"Of course," Tara replied confidently.

Dad was starting to feel a little braver and began asking a few questions, but Mum just sat there drinking her tea, as if a good cup of tea would make everything ok.

Diggie looked around him, watching all the smiling faces, and thinking what a nice planet this was, with so many young people. Mr Whisky-bee moved up close beside Diggie and blew on his nose, bringing him back from his daydream.

"Oh! Yes, Mr Whisky-bee. Now," he said.

And with that, a round packet with Tara's name on dropped from below his fluffy pillow cloud, followed by another one with Carlie's name on. Diggie picked them up and handed them to the children.

Tara was first to open hers, and she was thrilled.

Carlie looked just a little bewildered when he saw Tara's present, as he had started to tear off the paper, thinking it was a football. Once he realised it was a new lunch box, he smiled and said, "Thank you!"

The other children admired the boxes so much that Diggie asked Mr Whisky-bee if they could all have one, but Mr Whisky-bee had seen the children's excitement and was already spinning again.

He paused, then turned to Harry and asked, "What's your favourite planet?"

Harry looked puzzled. He was still only little, and knew nothing about planets.

Carlie's dad saw his predicament and said, "Earth, Harry, because that's the planet you live on."

"Earth! Earth!" shouted Harry.

And there it was – plop – one Earth planet packed lunch box.

"Now, Oliver, what about you?"

Oliver put his finger to his chin and squinted his eyes in deep thought. Finally, he said, "Harry has got Earth, Tara has got Mars, and Carlie has got Jupiter. I would like Mercury."

Mr Whisky-bee was only too happy to oblige. When Mark chose Pluto, Diggie explained it was only a dwarf planet, but Mark didn't seem to be listening.

Diggie said, "What about you, Hannah?"

She looked at Oliver's box, which seemed a little dark compared to the others, and said, "I know. The Sun!"

Mark laughed at his little sister. "Don't be silly!" he said, explaining to Hannah that the Sun is a star, not a planet.

"Well, now," said Diggie, "that would be a tall order. What do you think, Mr Whisky-bee?"

Mr Whisky-bee spun until he almost blew the trimmings off the tree. Then he stopped, looked at Hannah, and smiled.

"I think I've managed it," he told her. "What do you think?"

Hannah stood directly under Mr Whisky-bee as he began to lower her packed lunch box out of his cloud, and she was astonished to see the most beautiful box ever. Hannah's face lit up with the glow from her new gift, and her smile beamed from one ear to the other.

Everyone stared in amazement. It was just as though there was a piece of sunshine right in the middle of the room.

"Oh, well done," said Diggie.

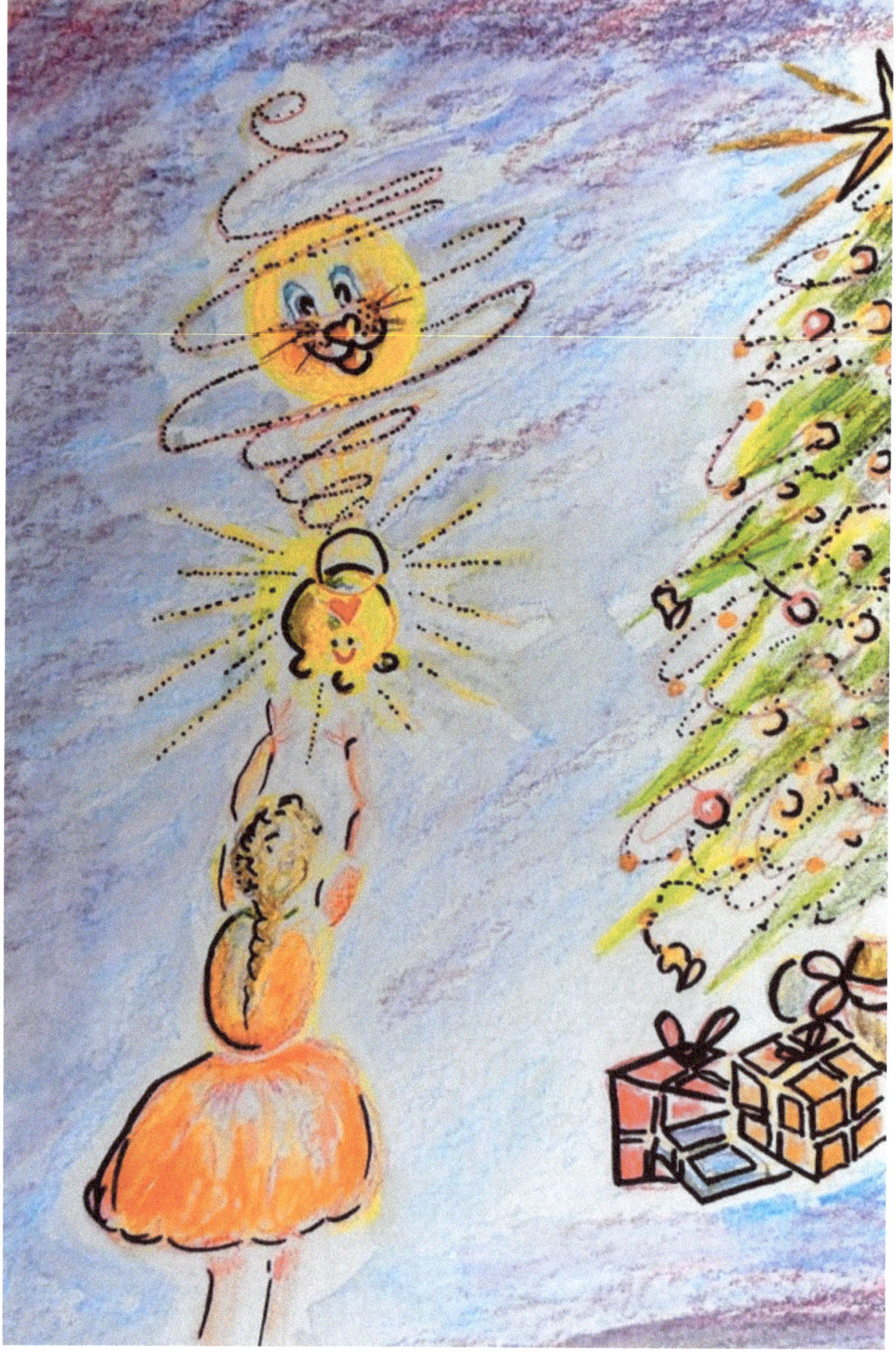

Mr Whisky-bee took a rest on his pillow. "Well, that wasn't easy," he sighed.

Suddenly Diggie hiccupped, and out of his mouth came a bubble in the shape of a heart, then another, and another. All the excitement had given him the hiccups, but the children had never seen hiccups in the shape of hearts before… or any shape. One went pop, but as it popped, it made such a noise that it sounded like a little beep. Each one made a different musical note, and the children started to jump up and down to pop them. And the more excited Diggie got, the more bubbles he hiccupped out.

The children's parents just smiled at each other, realising aliens were not so scary after all. After a while, Mark and his family went home and Carlie and Tara settled down to play with their new gifts. Mum was on her third mug of tea, still sitting – probably in shock – in her chair.

Mr Whisky-bee hovered over close to her and noticed that around her neck she wore a single stone (*And a very little stone at that*, he thought to himself.) It was hanging from a fine chain. As Mr Whisky-bee moved in for a closer look, Mum nervously shrank back into the chair, almost spilling what little was left of her tea.

Mr Whisky-bee's nose was almost touching the little rock that hung around her neck. He then pulled away and floated over to Dad, and they began to whisper something together. Mr Whisky-bee started to spin again.

Dad held out his hand, and Mr Whisky-bee dropped his new creation into it. Then Dad walked over to Mum.

"Look, dear. Look what Mr Whisky-bee has made for you!" Slowly he pulled one little rock after another out of his hand, each one a different colour and shape, until he had a whole necklace. He gently placed it around her neck.

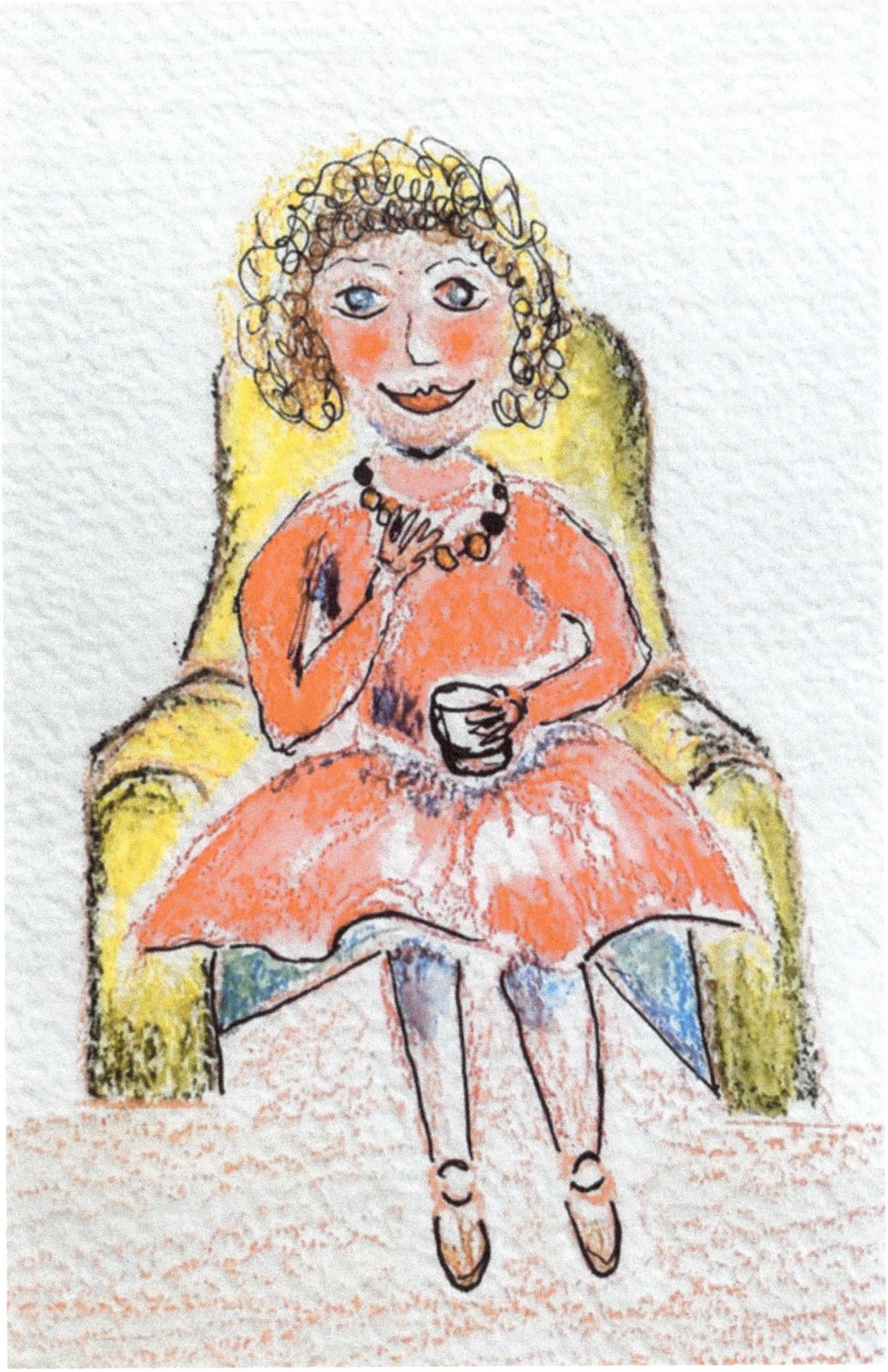

Mum drew in a big breath and put her hand on the lovely stones. "Oh, thank you!" she said. "Diggie and Mr Whisky-bee, would you care to stay for dinner?"

"That's it!" Carlie hugged Tara. "Mum's accepted them. We can keep them now."

"Don't be silly! You don't keep people," Tara stuttered. "I mean, spacemen."

As Mum made dinner, the children played with Mr Whisky-bee, and Diggie chatted away with Dad.

"So, Diggie," asked Dad, "do you have any plans, or will you be leaving soon?"

"Oh, no set plans. I was thinking that as I am here now, if you don't mind, I would like to do some exploring," replied Diggie.

Time passed quickly for the rest of that day. Later, when it was getting dark outside, Diggie asked the children's father if he would like to see his spaceship – an offer that Dad could not refuse.

But just as they left the house, Diggie looked up into the black sky and froze to the spot. He pointed to a large ball of silvery white light shining up above them.

"What's that?" he asked.

"Oh, that is the moon," replied Dad.

Diggie was puzzled. "What's a moon? Is it a planet or a star?" Diggie realised he had just found a new world to explore.

However, that's another story!

THE END

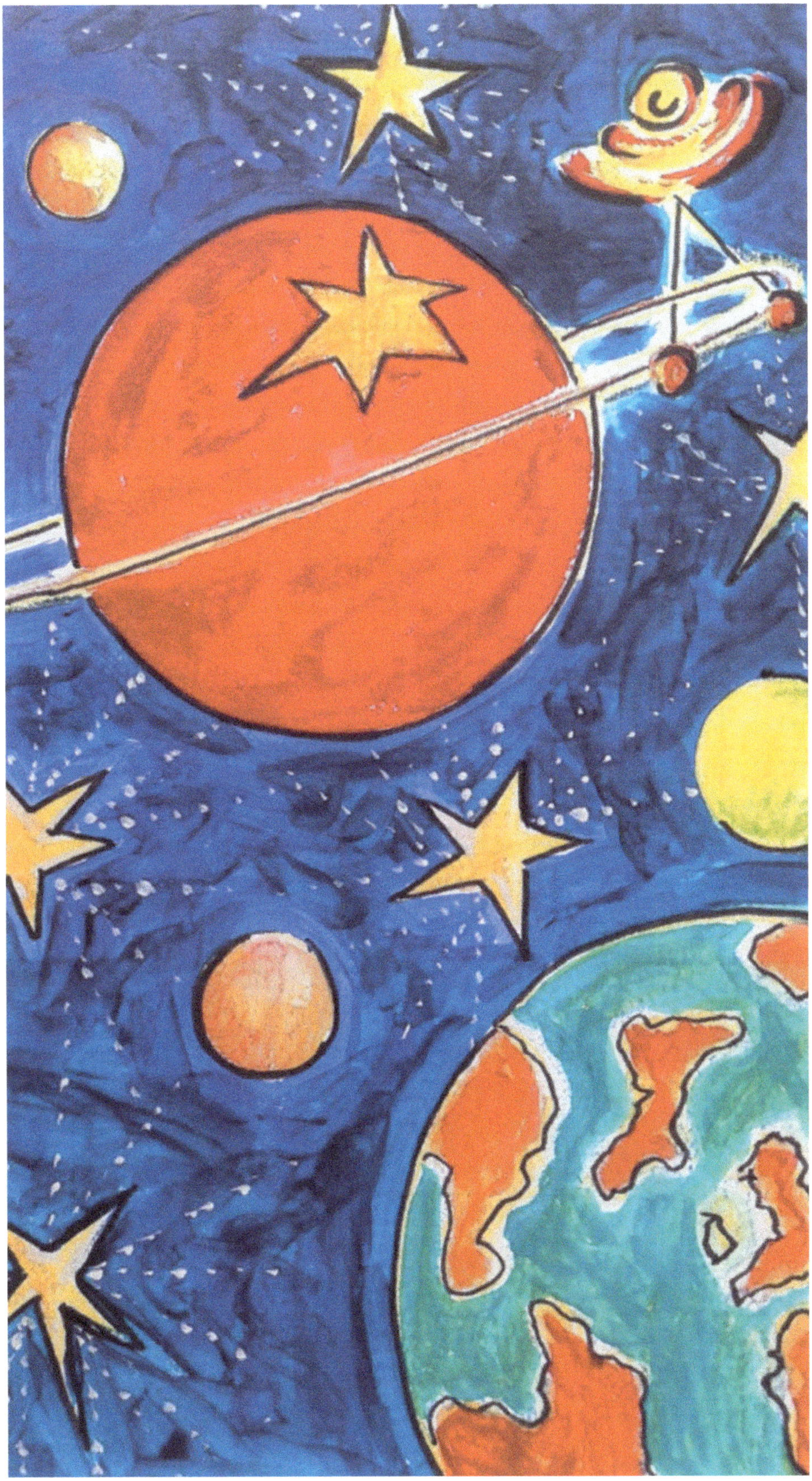

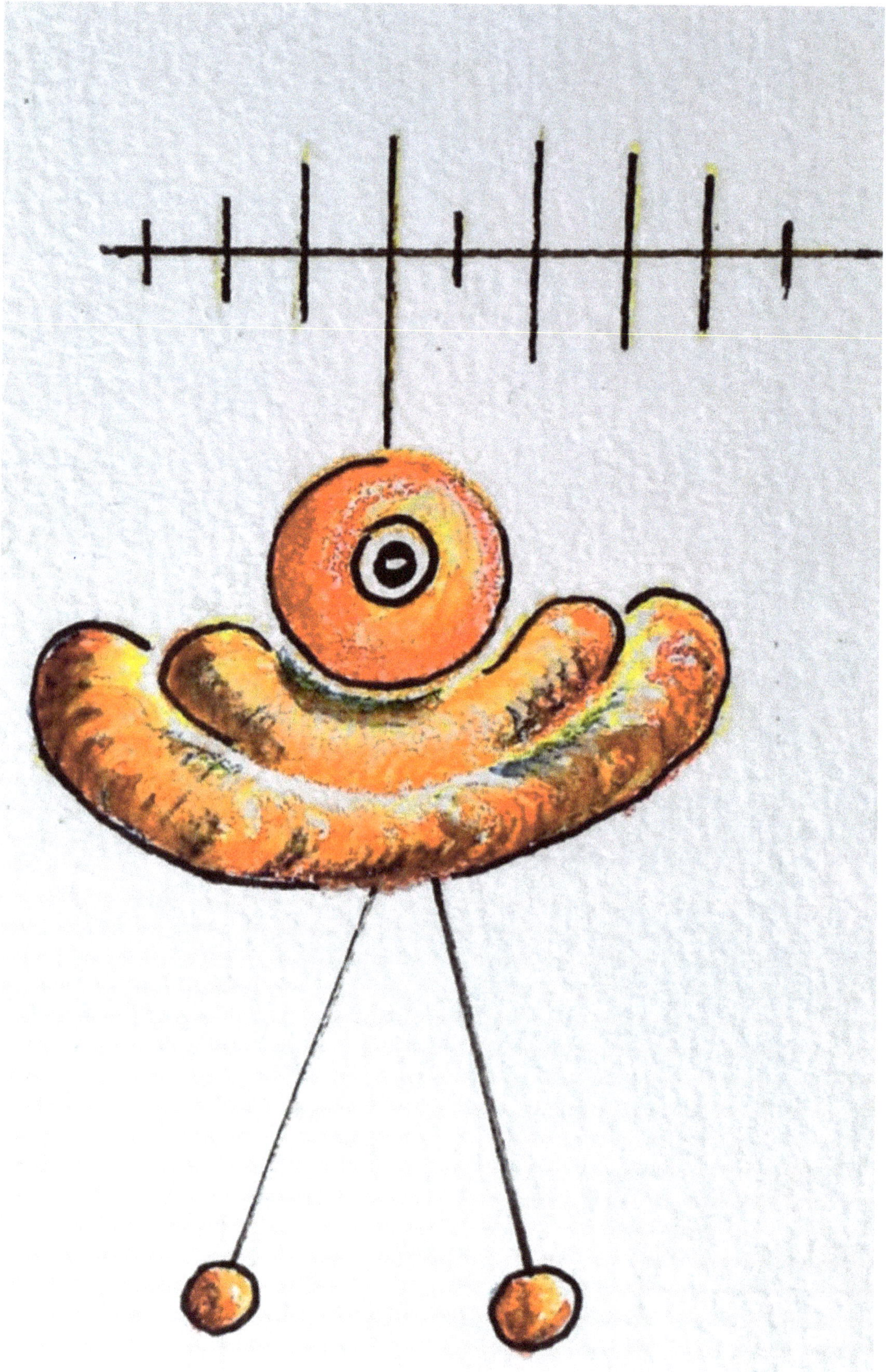

About the author

Sue Exton was born in Yorkshire, England, and now lives in North Lincolnshire. She studied watercolours with Eric Littlewood, a member of the Royal Academy. She works in all media, but recently has been working with the Derwent ink tense set of coloured pencils.

Ingram Content Group UK Ltd.
Milton Keynes UK
UKHW052358300323
419425UK00009B/94